New Maurston Primary School

D0333652

Stage Fright

Paul Stewart

Adapted by Gill Harvey

Illustrated by
Alan Marks

Reading Consultant: Alison Kelly
University of Surrey Roehampton

Contents

Chapter 1 Funny relatives   3

Chapter 2 At the Playhouse   13

Chapter 3 In a spin   21

Chapter 4 Mesmo's last act   27

Chapter 5 Isobel's story   32

Chapter 6 A fake letter?   39

Chapter 7 The mysterious book   44

Chapter 8 "Return!"   53

Chapter 9 The truth is out   59

Chapter 1

Funny relatives

Dom was lost. He was in the right village, but he couldn't find his uncle's house anywhere. "Excuse me. I'm looking for Mask Manor," he said politely to a passer-by.

The man pointed around a bend.

Keep going.
You can't miss it.

Dom went around the corner and peered down a spooky lane. Sure enough, black gates loomed ahead. The house behind them looked bleak and forbidding. He shivered. This didn't look like the "lovely house" his mother had described, when she arranged with his Uncle Charles for Dom to stay, all those months ago.

Taking a deep breath, Dom walked up to the gates. But as he was about to step through them, he was surrounded by squawking, ghostly birds.

The birds pecked at his face, before suddenly flying off.

Shaken, and wiping a drop of blood from his cheek, Dom rang the doorbell. A grim-looking woman opened the door and barked a question at him.

The woman stared at him. "Who am I?" she repeated, crossly. "I'm Eloise Bound, Giles Bound's wife."

"Well I'm Dominic, Charles and Giles' nephew," Dom said.

The woman frowned, then suddenly she seemed to remember. "Ah, Dom... Of course. Come in."

Mildred will show you your room.

Dom stepped into a gloomy hall. "Once you've unpacked, come to the dining room," his aunt snapped. "Dinner's in ten minutes."

A maid led Dom into a cold room with horrible, swirly wallpaper. He unpacked quickly, then ran downstairs to find everyone already seated.

Dom smiled nervously at the four people around the table. No one smiled back. One man didn't even seem to notice him.

8

"Meet your Uncle Giles," said his aunt, gesturing to the bald man next to Dom. Uncle Giles looked just as unfriendly as Aunt Eloise. But the man opposite his aunt seemed to be in a trance.

Aunt Eloise noticed Dom staring. "That's your Uncle Charles," she said, "and beside him is Isobel, his nurse."

Ignore Charles, he can't speak.

"He needs her to feed him," Aunt Eloise went on. "Charles had an accident on stage at the Playhouse last year. He's been like that ever since. Absolutely useless."

Eloise waved a hand dismissively and knocked her glass over.

The spreading stain on the cloth looked like blood, thought Dom.

As soon as he could, Dom escaped back to his room. Why hadn't his mother warned him his relatives were so strange?

Picking up his calculator, he tried to work out how much longer he had left in this terrible place.

I'm stuck here a week, so that's twenty-four hours times seven days...

But the calculator seemed to have a mind of its own. A series of numbers began to flash on the display. Dom frowned. The numbers made no sense at all...

...until he turned the calculator upside down. Grabbing a pen and paper, Dom wrote down each word as it appeared and read the message. What was going on?

ELOISE
LIES
GILES
LIES
SEE
ISOBEL

12

Chapter 2

At the Playhouse

The next morning, still confused, Dom decided to escape the manor and explore the village. In the very middle, he found a tall building with boarded-up windows.

Reading a poster pinned up outside, Dom realized the building was the Playhouse. Was this where Uncle Charles had his accident?

The poster showed a magician with scary eyes.

Mesmo's eyes drew Dom to the building. He wasn't sure why, but he just had to see inside.

Dom was wandering around the dusty seats when he heard a noise. Turning around, he saw his uncle's nurse, Isobel, in the doorway.

"Will you meet me at two o'clock in the summerhouse?" she asked.

Dom was puzzled, but before he could ask anything, she'd left.

He raced out after her. Isobel had vanished. Instead, he bumped into the stranger who'd helped him the night before.

It's you again! You were looking for Mask Manor...

Hello!

"Do you live here?" Dom burst out. "I need help. Everything's been so odd since I arrived..."

The man smiled kindly at Dom. "I'm not surprised," he said.

"Mask Manor has become an awful place since poor Charles had his accident and Giles came back." The man nodded at the Playhouse. "And that place is jinxed."

What do you mean?

Terrible things happened there.

"I used to work at the Playhouse," the man added. "I was in charge of the stage lighting for twenty years. My name's Larry Watkins."

"I'm Dominic," said Dom.
"Charles is my uncle. Do you know
what happened to him?"

"It's a long story," said Larry.
"Why not come back to my cottage
for a drink and I'll explain?"

Larry's cottage was crammed
with souvenirs from old plays –
including a giant pocket watch. As
Dom looked around, he saw a
newspaper cutting with Larry's
picture and began to read.

Close Shave for Young Actor

Rising star Simon Steele (25) was stabbed and seriously wounded in an accident on the Playhouse stage last night.

Larry Watkins

Eyewitness Larry Watkins told reporters, "The trick sword must have jammed. He's lucky to be alive."

The Playhouse, which was recently restored by Charles Bound of Mask Manor, is now closed until further notice.

"That was the start of the bad luck," said Larry, coming in suddenly with a tray, "and it was your Uncle Charles who stabbed the poor actor."

Asking Dom to sit down, he told him the whole story.

"The actor got such bad stage fright, he never acted again. Your uncle felt terrible. And then last year, when he finally reopened the Playhouse, he had his own accident on the first night."

Dom was about to ask about Charles' accident when a clock struck a quarter to two. He jumped up. "I'm sorry," he said quickly. "I have to go."

Chapter 3

In a spin

Dom raced to the summerhouse,
but there was no sign of Isobel.

"Maybe she isn't here yet," he
thought, stepping inside to look.

As Dom wondered how long to wait, he heard a knocking sound. Suddenly, the summerhouse was surrounded by birds.

They began to beat out a rhythm on the glass, their beaks endlessly tap-tap-tapping... louder... and louder...

Dom stared at the birds, his heart beating fast. The next thing he knew, the summerhouse itself began to turn. Around and around it flew, spinning faster and faster.

Help!
Hellllpppp!

Dom's head was in a daze. All he could see was whirling glass. Then something flew past him – a strange disc, carried by a tiny wren. Dom reached out for it...

...and was sucked into a long, dark tunnel. In the blackness, a tiny voice spoke in his ear.

"Help me! Help me come home!" the voice pleaded.

With a bump, Dom found himself lying on the floor of the summerhouse again, and a girl was sitting next to him.

Dom rubbed his head. What was Larry Watkins' granddaughter Abi doing in the summerhouse?

"I sometimes come and sit in here," Abi went on. "My grandad used to bring me here to play with Isobel's daughter Jenny."

Dom looked startled. "Isobel doesn't have a daughter."

"She did," Abi said sadly, "but no one has seen Jenny since that last night in the Playhouse. I must go," she added suddenly.

"Wait!" Dom called, but Abi had gone.

Chapter 4

Mesmo's last act

Dom went back to the manor, more baffled than ever. To his surprise, the place was completely deserted. This was his chance to look around. At the top of the house, he found a room full of pictures.

One of the pictures stood out. It showed a disc just like the one he'd seen in the summerhouse. As Dom stared at it, he felt as if he were falling into the picture...

The next thing he knew, he was inside the Playhouse. Mesmo the magician was on stage and a man and a girl were walking up to him.

The man looked like his Uncle Charles – but a happy, walking Charles. Then Dom noticed Isobel smiling in the front row. Perhaps the girl was her daughter Jenny.

A movement overhead made Dom look up. High above the stage, he could see Larry Watkins, working the lights. And someone else was running up behind him...

Back on stage, the magician was chanting in a low mumble. To Dom's surprise, Uncle Charles dropped down on all fours and began to howl like a wolf.

Dom looked around for Jenny, but he couldn't see her anywhere. Had Mesmo made her vanish?

He was peering into the shadows
when disaster struck. A sandbag
fell from the rafters, landing smack
on Mesmo's head.

As the magician slumped to the
floor, all the lights went out. The
performance was at an end.

Dom found himself back in Mask
Manor, his head spinning. At least
he now knew what was wrong with
his uncle. Charles was still in
Mesmo's trance.

Chapter 5

Isobel's story

The next morning, Abi came over again and Dom told her what he'd seen. Then they went to find Isobel.

"I'm sorry I wasn't at the summerhouse," Isobel apologized. "Charles needed me."

"But you aren't just my uncle's nurse, are you?" Dom asked.

You were at the Playhouse before the accident!

"I knew Charles several months before the accident," Isobel replied.

"We met one dark, stormy night when Jenny and I were lost in the car. We stopped at Mask Manor to ask for help."

"Charles was living alone. Since stabbing that poor actor, he'd shut himself away from the world. But he took us in for the night."

"Charles was so kind to us, we stayed on. He was lonely and my husband had died years before... Well, to cut a long story short, Charles and I fell in love."

"We decided to celebrate our engagement by opening the Playhouse for a variety show."

"On the night of the show, Mesmo asked for volunteers from the audience. So Charles and Jenny went on stage."

"Mesmo's first trick was to turn Jenny into a wren! I couldn't believe it."

"Then it was Charles' turn.
Mesmo hypnotized him – but the
sandbag hit him before he could
finish the act."

"I looked up and saw Larry
Watkins above the stage. He
must have dropped the sandbag!"

"The police took Larry away for questioning, but they couldn't prove anything."

Isobel's eyes filled with tears. "And now Charles is in a trance, Jenny has vanished and Giles and Eloise are awful."

Dom shook his head. It was a tragic story. But it didn't explain the birds – or any of the other odd things that had happened to him.

"I still don't understand," he said to Isobel. "I've been attacked by birds, sent back in time and I keep seeing this strange disc. What's going on?"

They're all Mesmo's doing.

"Mesmo is trying to put things right," Isobel told them.

"Mesmo?" exclaimed Abi. "I thought he was dead!"

38

Chapter 6

A fake letter?

Isobel looked uneasy. "I think Mesmo is contacting you from beyond the grave," she said. She looked desperately at Dom and Abi. "Will you help me rescue Charles and Jenny?"

What can we do?

"I don't know how yet," Isobel shrugged. "The problem is we don't have much time. Follow me. I have something to show you."

She led Dom and Abi to the library and took a letter from a secret drawer in the desk.

"Eloise 'found' this letter several months ago," Isobel explained. "I'm sure it's a fake, but I can't prove it."

Dom and Abi read the letter in silence.

If I have an accident, my brother Giles is to look after my affairs. If I am still not better after one year, everything I own will become his.
Signed: Charles Bound

Witnessed by: J Simmley

"How could Dom's uncle know he'd have an accident?" asked Abi.

"There's something fishy going on," agreed Dom.

"The year is up at six tonight," Isobel said gravely, "then Giles and Eloise will own Mask Manor."

A sudden howl echoed through the manor. "It's Charles," Isobel sighed. "Mesmo made him think he was a wolf. I'd better go."

HOOOOOWWWL

"I should go too," said Abi, so Dom walked with her to the gates. As he was walking back, a clock began to chime.

BONG! ... BONG! ... BONG! ...

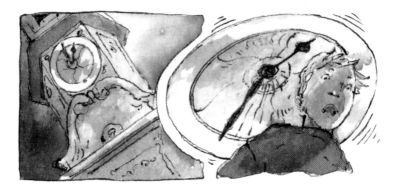

The clock struck the hour, but it kept on chiming. Dom couldn't block it out and with each chime he was forced to take a step. Soon, he found himself back at the Playhouse.

Chapter 7

The mysterious book

Still, Dom had no control over his feet. They led him down some steps, under the stage and into a dark, dusty room.

A light shone from a wardrobe in one corner. Dom flung open the doors...

...and saw a book. It was giving out an eerie glow and there was a very familiar pattern on the front.

"That's the pattern on the disc!" thought Dom.

Grabbing the book, he raced
from the Playhouse all the way
back to Mask Manor. Up in his
room, he opened it and sighed
with disappointment.

It's all in code!

Dom couldn't understand a
single word. In despair, he went
in search of Isobel.

"Oh dear," said Isobel. "Let me think." She frowned. "There is one more thing I can tell you, but I don't know if it will help. The sandbag that landed on Mesmo didn't kill him at once. He spent several days in the hospital saying the craziest things..."

"I think I know what he meant!" said Dom. "I'll be back soon."

He tore from the manor, heading straight for Larry Watkins' cottage and pounding on the door.

Mr. Watkins looked surprised to see him. He was even more surprised when Dom rushed to the living room and picked up the giant pocket watch.

"This is it," he cried. "This is *time that is upside down and back to front*."

Larry Watkins stared at Dom as though he was crazy. Just then, Abi came in.

Dom didn't notice. He'd managed to open the back of the watch and a folded sheet of paper had fluttered to the floor.

Dom snatched up the piece of paper. It was covered in symbols. "This must be the key to the book," he said. Seeing Larry and Abi's bewildered faces, he quickly told them about Mesmo's coded book.

A short time later, Dom and Abi lay on the floor of Dom's room with the book and the paper.

It still doesn't make any sense.

It must work somehow!

Suddenly, Abi gave a shout. "Dom, look!" She was sitting with the piece of paper in one hand and the book in the other. "When I hold them both together, the symbols in the book turn into English."

It's like magic!

Abi began reading. The book was full of spells. She'd just found one to bring someone out of a trance when Dom's Aunt Eloise burst in.

"What are you up to?" she snarled. "Some mischief, I'm sure. Just wait," she finished, as she turned to go. "After six tonight, things are going to change around here!"

Chapter 8

"Return!"

There was no time to waste. It was five o'clock already.

"We have to take Charles back to the Playhouse to cure him," said Abi. Clutching the book and the paper, they raced to find Isobel.

Soon, they were all in her car and Isobel sped away.

The car screeched to a halt outside the Playhouse and they dragged Charles inside. Abi stood in front of him, holding the book and paper. Slowly, she began to chant.

Dom and Isobel stood to one side and held their breath...

Then Abi shouted out, "Return!" and Uncle Charles jumped. He blinked once or twice and looked around in delight.

"I'm back!" he said, amazed.

Charles frowned. "Where's Jenny?"

Abi flipped through the book. "I think I know how to rescue her too," she muttered. She chanted a second spell and the Playhouse filled with birds.

"They've brought her!" cried Dom, spotting a wren.

"Return!" Abi shouted again, and all of a sudden there was Jenny herself.

"We must get back to the manor now," Dom said urgently.

Charles looked at him curiously. "What's the hurry?" he asked.

"Dom's right," Isobel broke in. "If we don't get back before six, Charles, you'll lose everything."

I'll explain on the way.

Then to the manor!

They arrived just in time. Uncle Giles' hand was hovering over the paper about to sign. In seconds, Mask Manor would be his.

Uncle Charles burst into the study. "Stop!" he shouted. Then he stared at Giles in astonishment. "You're not my brother," he said.

Chapter 9

The truth is out

Charles towered over Giles and
Eloise. "My brother Giles lives in
India," he went on. "You're Simon
Steele, the actor I stabbed on stage
all those years ago."

"And you're not Aunt Eloise," Charles added, turning to the woman behind Giles. "I've never seen you before in my life."

The woman glared at him. "I'm Simon's wife," she spat, "and you ruined his career."

I hate you!

"I was the one who dropped the sandbag on Mesmo. But I wanted to kill you, not the magician."

Dom and Abi looked at each other. At last everything made sense. With Charles hypnotized, Simon and his wife had forged a letter to steal Mask Manor and all the money. They had almost succeeded, too.

Just then, a violent rumbling shook the manor.

"What's happening?" Abi yelled at Dom. "Is it an earthquake?"

Dom thought quickly. "Let go of Mesmo's book," he suggested.

Abi dropped it and the book began to spin around, whirling into a blur. With a bang, it disappeared and the room became still.

Isobel smiled. "Mesmo knows his work is done," she said. "Now, he can rest in peace."

A week later, the Playhouse was opened once more, for a very special production – Charles and Isobel's wedding.

Simon Steele and his wife didn't attend. They were behind bars. But there was one surprise guest. The real Uncle Giles flew in from India to join them.